For Matilda, with love - H. W.

For Cain - W. A.

A Templar Book

First published in the UK in hardback in 2004 by Templar Publishing.
This softback edition first published in 2005 by Templar Publishing,
an imprint of The Templar Company plc,
Pippbrook Mill, London Road, Dorking, Surrey, RH4 1JE, UK
www.templarco.co.uk

Text copyright © 2004 by Helen Ward
Illustration copyright © 2004 by Wayne Anderson

First softback edition, third impression

ISBN - 13: 978-1-84011-519-2
ISBN - 10: 1-84011-519-X

Designed by Mike Jolley
Edited by A. J. Wood

Printed in China

HELEN WARD

Twenty-five December Lane

Illustrated by WAYNE ANDERSON

templar publishing

It had been a long and dreary
December. And here it was — Christmas Eve.
For weeks one small shopper had been searching
for the perfect present . . .
to give to someone very special.

No matter where she looked,
she couldn't find it.

The main street was noisy

and crowded with fast and furious people.

The girl was stepped on . . .

pushed and jostled...

and squeezed off the busy
pavement...

...into the damp gloom of

December Lane,

which was as grey and as cold and as empty

as winter without Christmas.

❦

Wind-chased rubbish
rattled around her feet as she shivered
and peered into the shabby shop windows.

Windows full of spare parts and ancient electricals . . .
huge hideous underwear (almost, but not quite, pink);
windows that were empty but for uncollected post
and dead insects.

On she went, when any ordinary shopper
would have turned back.

Just as the girl was about to give up and go home,
a glimmer from across the street caught her eye.

❧

At Number Twenty-Five
she found just what she was after.
It was the strangest shop she had ever seen
and she couldn't recall having seen it before.
As she pushed open the narrow door,
a bell on a spring rang.

A little breath of Christmas

slipped past her, out into December Lane
and up to the dark grey clouds.

❧

She closed the door carefully behind her
and stood staring in wonder.

She had never seen

so many toys!

Teddy bears and clockwork cars,

teepees, castles, Noah's Arks,

books and dolls and dinosaurs

disappeared into the distance.

There was a kerfuffle at one of the counters.

Another customer was being served.

Shop assistants bustled past.

"Excuse me," said the girl politely.

"I'd like to buy a . . ."

"I'll be with you shortly," came the answer.

❧

The Other Customer,

who just fitted into his old grey coat
and worn-out hat, was busy
scooping games from the shelves
into a sack.

"Can you help me?"
the girl asked a hurrying assistant.
"I see you have a . . ."

"Won't be a moment," he replied.

Up and down the ladders the assistants flew
as the Other Customer pointed and nodded
at the things he wanted.

"Oh dear," said the girl as one
shelf after another became empty.
"Surely he's not going to buy
everything?"

But the passing assistant just
waved a dismissive hand.

The toys continued to roll and
scuttle into the enormous sack.
They rattled and pinged
and squeaked and whistled
until the floor, the ceiling,
the long, long counter and every shelf
was cleared into the bulging sack
as if **by magic.**

The girl looked on in dismay.

"Oh please," she said.

"Not that one . . ."

MAGIC

But it was too late . . .

The Other Customer was ready to leave.

He tied his great sack shut, slung it over his back
and somehow squeezed through the narrow door,
leaving just enough space for a loud

"*Merry Christmas.*"

As he bustled away, the girl
thought she caught the wink of a kind and twinkly eye.
Then the chief assistant finally turned to her and said

"I'm very sorry, Miss,
but we have nothing left to sell."
"Oh dear," said the girl, feeling her heart sink.
She opened the door just enough, and slipped
back out into December Lane.

Her feet stepped out onto sparkling new snow.

She looked up into the darkness,

now thick with swirling snowflakes, and smiled.

How happy this first snow would make that

special someone waiting for her at home.

It wasn't a gift she had bought in a shop,

but it was still something she could share.

❧

Then out of the sky
something tumbled toward her . . .

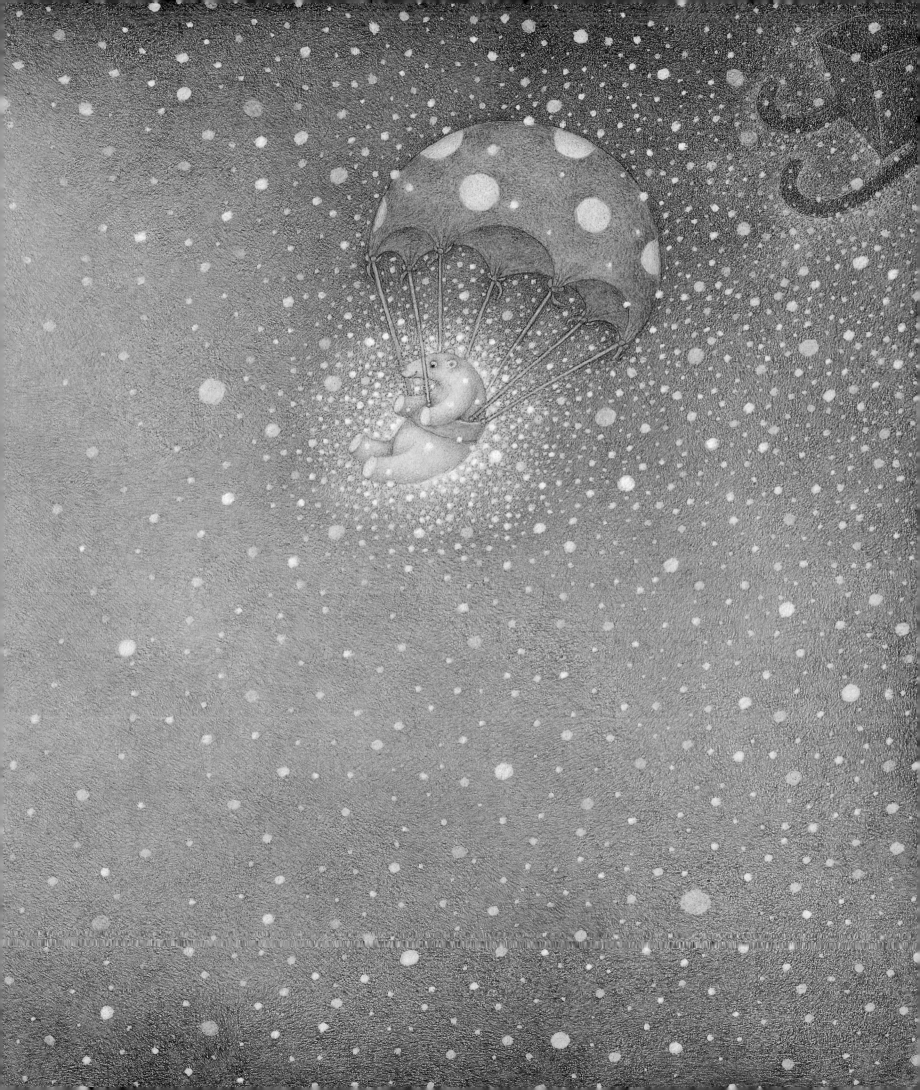

With a flurry and a gentle thud,

a little breath of Christmas

landed at her feet.

❧

It was perfect!

And it was exactly what she

had been searching for!

A very special present indeed . . .

for **someone** *very special.*